A Fall Ball for All

This one's for Jon
—J.S.

To my beloved Alberto and my dearest
children Gabriele and Margherita
—C.F.

Millbrook Press
A division of Lerner Publishing Group, Inc.
241 First Avenue North
Minneapolis, MN 55401 USA

For reading levels and more information, look up this title at www.lernerbooks.com.

Designed by Danielle Carnito.
Main body text set in Dinkle Bold 22/24. Typeface provided by Chank.
The illustrations in this book were done with mixed media (watercolor, colored pencils, and tempera) with digital retouching.

Library of Congress Cataloging-in-Publication Data

Names: Swenson, Jamie A., author. | Fedele, Chiara, illustrator.
Title: A fall ball for all / Jamie A. Swenson ; illustrated by Chiara Fedele.
Description: Minneapolis : Millbrook Press, (2018) | Summary: "The autumn wind invites all the creatures of the forest
   to its Windfall Ball. At the ball, they'll celebrate the end of autumn and the coming of winter with a grand feast."
   —Provided by publisher.
Identifiers: LCCN 2017043610 (print) | LCCN 2017055550 (ebook) | ISBN 9781512498035 (lb : alk. paper) |
   ISBN 9781541523722 (eb pdf)
Subjects: | CYAC: Stories in rhyme. | Autumn—Fiction. | Winds—Fiction. | Forest animals—Fiction. | Balls (Parties)—Fiction.
Classification: LCC PZ8.3.S99558 Fal 2018 (print) | LCC PZ8.3.S99558 (ebook) | DDC (E)—dc23

LC record available at https://lccn.loc.gov/2017043610

Manufactured in the United States of America
1-43530-33328-1/25/2018

A Fall Ball for All

JAMIE A. SWENSON

ILLUSTRATED BY
CHIARA FEDELE

MILLBROOK PRESS
MINNEAPOLIS

Once upon a golden day,
Autumn Wind blew in to play,
Whooshing leaves into the air—
Orange, brown, purple everywhere.

At every burrow, den, and nest
An invitation fell to rest:

Geese postponed their grand migration,
Bears and bats, their hibernation.

Excitement for the party grew,
From Great Gray Owl
to smallest shrew.

The creatures donned their autumn best—
Fur and feather primped and pressed.

Coyote groomed, Pheasant preened,
Porcupine shook, Otter cleaned.

The nights grew longer into fall
As Autumn Wind prepared the ball.

Squalls sent pumpkins tumbling 'round.
A breeze shook apples to the ground.

Gusts and gales and tempest forces
Set a fete with seven courses:

Cranberries, chestnuts, corn, and plums,
Sunflowers, daisies, chrysanthemums.

Harvest Moon set the night aglow.
Guests arrived—some fast, some slow—

With time to nibble, greet, and play
While festive tunes got under way.

Rabbit and Turtle tapped a beat
As Wind composed an Autumn Suite.

Soon the night was filled with song.
A blustery chorus sang along.

Then Autumn Wind began to dance—
It breezed,
it blew,
it puffed,
it pranced.

Beckoning both big and small
To join in step at the Windfall Ball.

Turkey strutted with Elk and Quail.
Beaver kept time with his tail—

A swirling night of celebration,
Windy, joyful jubilation.

In the shindig's happy wake,
An autumn treasure for all to take:

A Windfall feast, a winter's cache
To gobble, bury, store, or stash.

Chipmunks filled their furry cheeks.

Raccoons took pumpkins, corn, and leeks.

Then Badger raised one final toast
For all who gathered and their host.

And every burrow, hill, and nest
Was ready then for winter's rest.

Autumn waved goodbye to all—
Until the next year's Windfall Ball.

wind·fall

1: fruit or other crops blown down by the wind

2: an unexpected gift or good fortune

A windfall is a special treat for creatures in nature. It could be fruit blown down from trees, made much easier for animals to gather. Or, as in this story, it could be a whole pile of food to last through a long winter. And sometimes a windfall means a sudden bit of good luck, even for people.

AUTHOR'S NOTE

The animals at the Windfall Ball represent those found in the Northwoods of the United States. In Wisconsin, where I live, autumn is a time for harvesting the fruits of the warm season and preparing for a long, cold winter. Warm-blooded animals may have adapted to survive the winter weather, or they may hibernate or migrate to warmer areas until the snow and ice melt away. But whether they stash food away or eat more in fall to fatten up, the animals must find enough food to sustain themselves until spring.

Fall has always felt like a celebration to me, as leaves turn bright colors and the season's last fruits and vegetables ripen. There are few things I enjoy more than hiking on a crisp autumn day as leaves and petals dance in the wind and squirrels scurry about preparing for the winter. It wasn't hard for me to imagine a wonderful Windfall Ball somewhere deep in the woods to carry on that celebration. Now, if only I could find my invitation!